The Wind in the Willows

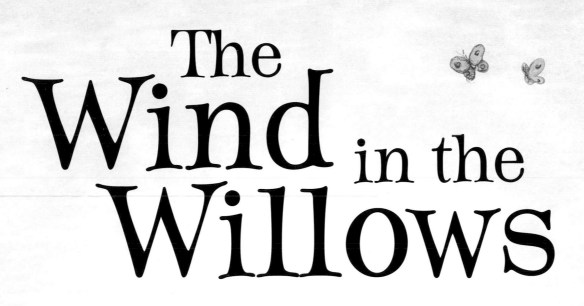

Illustrated by Mauro Evangelista

Retold by Lesley Sims

Based on the original story by Kenneth Grahame

Ratty and Mole were out for a row,
just messing about on the river.

With a **splish** and a **splash**,
Otter's head popped up.

"Hello you two!" he gurgled.
"Toad is looking for you."

Toad Hall stood grand and tall, right on the edge of the river.

Ratty rowed there at once.

"You're here!" Toad cried. "Come for a ride in my brand new caravan."

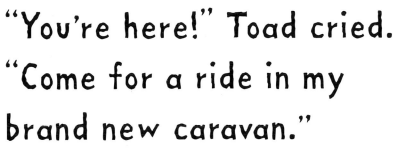

They rambled along the country lanes, talking of this and of that.

Insects were humming and birds were chirping, when...

Poop! Poop!

A sports car shot past in a cloud of smoke, sending everyone flying.

"Scoundrels!" shouted Ratty.

"Villains!" muttered Mole.

"Poop! Poop!" said Toad. "Forget that boring old caravan. I'm buying a car."

From that moment, Toad was hooked.
Cars were all he could think about.

He drove them, he dreamed about
them and he cheered when
he saw a new one.

So Ratty and Mole amused themselves.
They played hide-and-seek in the
Wild Wood...

...or stayed with
their friend, Badger.

"How's Toad?" asked Badger one night, over cookies and cocoa. "Still buying new cars?"

"Buying them and crashing them," said Ratty. "He's the World's Worst Driver."

"We'll have to help him," Badger declared. "Tomorrow, we'll pay him a visit..."

"Hello you fellows!" said Toad, early the next morning. "I'm just off for a drive."

"Oh no you're not," said Badger.
"You're a menace on the road.
We're taking your keys and
keeping you inside."

"It's for your own
good Toad," added Mole.

"They won't stop me!" Toad chuckled, as he escaped. "I'll find a car to drive."

Soon he saw the perfect one. As if in a dream, he clambered in... ...and sped away.

That night, Toad was in prison.
"Oh, why did I steal a car?"
he thought.

"Oh clever Badger, oh sensible Mole,
oh
foolish,
foolish
Toad."

Toad was down – but not for long.

Late one night, he escaped
from prison, cunningly
disguised as a
washerwoman.

When the moon was high in the sky,
he curled up by a tree and
snuggled into his shawl.

He fell asleep, dreaming of home.

But back at Toad Hall - calamity! His home had been stolen from him by stealthy stoats and wicked weasels.

"Don't panic, Toad," said Mole.
"Badger has a plan."

And Badger did, for he knew of a secret
tunnel that would take them right
into Toad Hall.

In the dead of night, armed with sticks and swords, they followed Badger down the secret tunnel...

...and burst out into the kitchen.

"CHARGE!" hollered Badger.

What a squealing and a screeching
filled the air.
"Take my house would you? Take that!"
shouted Toad.

WHAM!

The stoats and the weasels were
banished forever. Toad was so thrilled,
he held a small party to celebrate.

And he never drove another car again.

Edited by Jenny Tyler
Designed by Hannah Ahmed
Digital manipulation by Mike Wheatley